AF485224

Skye Travels Airborne

A Short Story

The Worthingtons

Kathryn Kaleigh

Skye Travels Airborne

Noah Worthington ran a hand along a wall in the large abandoned building. Little flakes of steel gray paint fluttered to the cracked concrete floor.

Someone had left a coffee cup, still filled with stale coffee on one of the exposed beams.

The one-story windowless building was big, big enough anyway. About the size of a basketball court.

It smelled dusty and stale, but the open door let in the scent of jet fuel from the tarmac. The tarmac that was just outside the door. As in walk out the door onto the tarmac.

The deep roar of jet engines filled the silence.

Savannah stood in the middle of the room, looking toward the open door leading out onto the tarmac.

Noah's wife. They'd been married for two months and he still had trouble believing it. Sometimes he wondered if he had cheated her by whisking her off to Las Vegas for a small wedding. But her mother and sister had been there.

By essentially eloping, they had avoided the necessary evil of having to invite Noah's family. God help them all if that had happened.

She was so beautiful that just looking at her made his heart tremble.

Feeling him watching her, she turned and smiled.

"It doesn't look like much, does it?" Noah asked.

"No," she said. "But Noah, it could be something."

He thought so, too, but he wanted to hear it from her. Needed to hear it from her.

"It needs a lot of work," he said, pointing out the obvious.

"What kind of roof does it have?" Savannah asked.

"Roof?" Not the kind of question he was expecting. "I don't know."

"Is it a flat roof?" Looking up toward the ceiling, she turned in a slow circle, her flowy skirt fluttering in the breeze that came in through the door. "I think it must have some steel beams."

"I think it's flat," I said. "It has to be flat."

The building was an old hangar from back in the early days of the Houston airport. When it was still called Houston Intercontinental Airport. This particular building, in fact, had been the hub of scheduled helicopter airline services operated by Executive Helicopters.

The building had been vacant since Executive Helicopters had ceased to operate out of the airport.

"It was the helicopter building," he told her.

Savannah was still looking at the ceiling with a look in her eyes he recognized.

Smiling, she turned and looked at him.

"Noah," she said. "It's on the tarmac."

"I know."

"How did you even find it?" She kept talking before he even got the chance to answer.

"It's perfect. Not this," she said, waving a hand dismissively.

"I don't understand. Do you mean tear it down?"

"No. Use it as a walk through area. Maybe even some covered parking. Build a second floor. A really nice second floor. With an elevator."

"Why?" he asked, knowing she had a vision, but he was struggling to see it.

She walked over to him, took his hands and looked into his eyes.

"The view," she said simply. "A second floor with floor-to-ceiling windows. A lobby. A receptionist. Offices. Your office—a corner office—looking out over the tarmac."

Noah could see it now. Everything she was describing.

"How is it you know so much?" Noah asked.

"My father was an engineer," she said as though that explained everything.

"I think..." he said, cupping her cheeks in his hands. "I think it's more than that. I think it's just your inquisitive mind. You absorb things. Like a sponge."

"Every wife wants to be compared to a sponge."

Noah laughed, feeling happiness swelling in his heart.

"Actually sea sponges are unassuming creatures. Even though they can't even move, they survive and are some of longest surviving animals on the planet. Did you know that the treatment for leukemia comes from a sponge?"

"And you asked me how I know so much," she said, standing on her toes to plant a quick kiss on his lips.

"A pilot has a lot of time to read."

"Most people would read novels. My husband reads about sponges. And worse, he remembers it."

My arms still loosely around her waist, I moved her in a slow swaying movement.

"And my wife thinks about adding second floors to old buildings."

Slipping out of my arms, she went to the door looking out at the tarmac.

I followed, standing behind her.

"This could be the start of something big," she said. "I can feel it. How many more airplanes can you afford to buy? It doesn't matter. We'll make it work."

"It means moving to Houston," Noah said.

"I like Houston. We'll buy a house. A big one."

"A high rise," Noah said.

She turned in his arms and looked up into his eyes.

"No. I'm thinking a house. A real house. With lots of rooms. A big backyard."

"Why do we need all that room?" Noah asked.

She spun out of his arms again and stepped outside onto the tarmac, the wind tousling her long brunette hair.

"There's something I want to talk to you about."

Automatic fear slammed into his gut.

"What did I do?"

"It's not about you, silly."

"Then what's it about?" He watched her carefully. Savannah had a way of throwing out ideas that could bend a man's thoughts like a pretzel. It was one of the many, many things he loved about her.

She took a deep breath, but didn't look at him.

"I want to go back to school. I want to be a psychologist."

"Okay," I said. "You've mentioned something about that before." Noah glanced at his watch for the date. "It's too late to apply for this year, but you can start next year."

"Getting into graduate school is a lot harder than getting into undergrad."

"I know. Do you want me to help you?"

Even though Noah's father and he weren't on speaking terms, the Worthington name still carried weight when used in certain circles. Noah wouldn't use it for his own gain, but he would use it for Savannah. He would do anything for her.

She turned and smiled at him. Her smile was brighter than the Houston sunlight.

"I've already been accepted for this Fall."

"What? Where?"

"Three schools. One of them is the University of Houston. I haven't accepted yet."

"How did you know? What made you apply here? You have to accept it."

"I know. I will."

"It's all coming together, isn't it?" Noah asked. "Our life."

She closed the distance between them and wrapped her arms around him, squeezing him in a hug that said everything.

"You have to buy it," she said, glancing back up at the roof. "The building."

An airplane left the runway, its loud engines momentarily blocking their conversation.

Together they watched the airplane as it left the runway and took to the clear blue skies.

Noah's own little Cessna sat a few feet away. It had seen better days, that was for sure. Even though he'd bought it used, it was his. Noah's very first airplane.

Already, he had passengers—paying passengers—at least twice a week. Just last week, he'd had four. Word was getting around.

He swept a hand over her cheek and grinned.

"I already bought it."

"What?"

She pushed away from him. "You're incorrigible."

"And that's why you love me."

"I love you despite it," she said, but she was smiling.

"But..." Noah said. "It didn't occur to me to put a second floor on the building."

"You still need me," she said.

He took her hands, clasped them with hers.

"I will always need you."

He brought her hands up to his lips to kiss her palms.

"What's this?" he asked.

"What?"

She was wearing the O-ring he had used to propose to her when they were in college. The first time he had proposed. Before they had split up.

"You kept this?"

"Of course I kept it."

Noah wasn't sure if he was surprised that she had kept it or if he was more surprised that she was wearing it.

It was hard to say. He was surprised about both.

He lifted her other hand.

"You have a proper ring." Noah referred to the perfect Tiffany diamond ring on her finger with the matching wedding band.

"I know. And it's beautiful. But I can like this one, too. It has special meaning for me."

"I love you, Savannah Skye."

"I know."

"Do you think—" Noah stopped. Looked up toward the blue sky with white wispy clouds.

"Do I think what?" she asked.

"I just had a thought."

"Oh boy."

"No. Really. It's a good one. It..." Noah looked down at the love of his life. "It's perfect.

"Well," Savannah said. "Tell me."

"I have the perfect name for our airline."

"Worthington Enterprises," she said.

Noah shook his head. "This is so much better."

"Well…"

"We'll name it Skye Travels."

She looked at him. Blinked.

Skye was Savannah's middle name. It was perfect.

Noah was surprised he hadn't thought of it already.

"Skye Travels?"

"It's perfect."

She kissed him on the lips.

"You don't mind?"

"I love it. It's perfect. How could I mind?"

"Oh," Noah said, watching a small jet coming in for a landing. That. That was what he wanted. He'd have a whole fleet of them.

"You might mind because your name will be plastered across all our airplanes."

"If I was narcissistic, it might bother me," she said. "But I'm not shy. Besides, no one will know our company was named after me."

"We'll know."

"Wait," she said, looking at me sideways. "Are you going to spell it S-k-y or S-k-y-e?"

"What do you think?"

"With the 'e.' Otherwise, it's just ordinary."

"Wouldn't have the same meaning anyway, would it?" Noah pulled her close and kissed her on the nose. "Happy?" he asked.

"Yes. While we're in the mood for naming things, it might be a good time to name… something else."

"What else?" Noah asked. "Some people name their airplanes, but I don't think that's necessary. Do you?"

"No. I do not. But that's not what I was going to suggest we name." She was watching him carefully.

"Oh. Then. What do we need to name?"

"We could start picking out names for our first child."

"Our first... Why would?... Are you?"

She nodded, biting her lip in a little smile.

"We're going to have a baby?"

She nodded.

Picking her up at the waist, he twirled her around until they were both laughing with dizziness.

"We're having a baby," Noah said, a wide grin across his face. "I hope we have a girl who looks just like you."

"Or a boy who looks like you."

"Let's have one of each. Or two of each. Let's have—"

"Let's not get carried away, Noah Worthington. Just because you plan to have a fleet of airplanes does not mean that we need to have a fleet of children."

"How did you know I wanted to have a fleet of airplanes?"

"Because I know you Noah Worthington. You're one of the most ambitious men I've ever met and I've met a lot of ambitious men."

"Is there a compliment in there somewhere?"

"Nothing but."

Noah took her hand and they walked toward the little Cessna that he had bought used. It was a good plane to start with.

Skye Travels.

It was a good name.

"I'm going to take care of you, Savannah," Noah said.

"I know. And I'm going to take care of you."

"No. I mean I'm really going to take care of you."

He helped her climb into the copilot's seat of the Cessna and buckled her in.

She knew how to buckle herself in. She knew he knew she knew. But it was a ritual they had started long ago.

He buckled her in, gave her a kiss, and they were off.

The sun reflected off the tarmac and they taxied toward the runway.

With the sun just right, Noah could see it.

He could see the deserted, halfway dilapidated building turned into a two-story private terminal.

The second floor would be all windows on this side. It would have a view of the tarmac. When he wasn't flying in a plane, he could watch airplanes landing and taking off.

With Savannah at his side, they could do anything.

Noah Worthington's life was unfolding before him.

Gaining ground effect just like the little Cessna as he took them into the air.

Keep Reading for a Preview of Begin Again...

KATHRYN KALEIGH

Begin Again

THE WORTHINGTONS

Preview

Chapter 1

Savannah Richards didn't believe in chance.

But there he stood, head bent, focused on his iPad. Handsome in his black uniform - black tie, white shirt, silver stripes at his wrists. A captain's cap sitting atop his head His hair graying around the edges.

Noah wouldn't recognize her now – even if he remembered her.

He would be forty-two now. A far cry from the college senior who had been attached to her hip for a year. He'd been a boy then, but his features were the same. A few pounds heavier, but that was to be expected. The five o'clock shadow that never failed to appear by early afternoon. The same brow that she had seen furrowed over a calculous problem seemed to have made a permanent home between his eyes. No wonder, as he had worn it often. Sometimes even as he'd studied her, though he thought she hadn't known.

As a college senior, the only time he'd left her side was when he was flying or training to fly. Sometimes she'd gone with him to practice on the simulator. She usually ended up using the time to study her own biology textbooks or read an English lit novel. Side by side, each lost in their own world.

The time, she thought wryly, had been well spent. After her freshman year, Savannah had immersed herself in her studies and graduated top of her class with a bachelor's degree in science.

Noah also had displayed a singular passion – aviation. And everything that went with it. Flying. Airplanes. Weather reports. When he hadn't been engrossed in aviation, however, he'd turned that singular focus on her. The memory brought a flush to her cheeks.

And a familiar stab to her heart.

As the terminal train arrived at the station and the door opened to allow people to exit, it occurred to her that she could take six steps to the left, get in his train car, and speak to him. It was a much more logical thing to do than just watching him – letting him breeze by her.

Two ships passing in the night.

No. He was a ship from the past. She would let him go.

She was still mad at him.

. . .

Noah Worthington glared at the flight schedule displayed on his iPad and wondered if his lunch had not agreed with him. The terminal train at Atlanta airport was interminably slow. He wasn't sure if he wanted it to hurry up or to never arrive. He struggled to find a middle ground.

He was seeing an apparition. He knew it had to be a vision because the girl he recognized wore a snug red pencil skirt with matching suit jacket. Her black pumps, though, had a matching red bottom. She carried a black leather Louis Vuitton handbag in a cross-body style, freeing up her hands. He recognized the LV twist-lock on the front – its only readily identifiable feature. The silver on the handbag matched the buttons on her suit. And the gray of her camisole. Her long brunette hair fell in loose waves around her face. Her make-up was flawless down to the shiny, but muted glossy red lipstick.

The college freshman from his indelible memory wore jeans ripped at the knees, white canvas sneakers, and either a sweatshirt or t-shirt depending on the weather. She'd kept her hair pulled back in a loose ponytail. The only time he'd seen her dressed up was when she wore a dark gray cardigan and matching shell with black slacks to a dinner with his family. She'd worn low heeled dark gray moto boots. He'd been impressed, at the time, at how put together and cute she looked. Her hair had fallen straight to her shoulder and though he hadn't commented, he'd known she had taken the time to straighten it with a flat iron. Her hair was naturally wavy and thick and she hated it. Hence, the ponytail.

All in all, perhaps that was a precursor to the woman who

watched him now. Or perhaps she was his mind's rendition of the girlfriend he'd so inconsiderately left behind twenty years ago. Besides, what college freshman gained no more than a couple of pounds and in all the right places after twenty years?

The vision watched him, though she didn't know he knew. He recognized the expression she wore.

She was still mad at him.

The train rolled in, the door opened, and throngs of people rushed out of the cars. She got into the car behind his, moving with that same lilt in her step that even he hadn't managed to dull.

She's only a vision. Probably some random girl from California who just happened to have similar – very similar facial features.

However, he knew the saying that one never forgot his first love to be true.

He glanced at the time on his tablet. He had time for dinner before his flight, now delayed, took off for Dallas. He didn't feel like going to the officer's club. Didn't feel like talking aviation. Or hearing about someone's new aircraft acquisition. He just wanted to enjoy some peaceful time to read his novel, order a martini he wouldn't drink, and have a meal.

He scanned his ID and slipped into the Diner's Club – away from the other pilots. He wasn't exactly nondescript in his pilot's uniform, but he'd learned over the years that the typical flyer tended to not bother the pilots. He'd never quite discerned if it was out of respect, awe, or fear. Perhaps just disinterest. Whatever it was, he'd grown to count on it when he wanted to be left alone.

He took a small table for two near the bar, his back to the room. He found it less distracting to read when he couldn't see people hurrying to and fro.

He ordered a sandwich and water. And resumed his attention on the novel he read on his iPad. It was about a man who never slept. In theory, he liked the concept, but in reality, sleep was one of his favorite pastimes.

And allowed the world to fade into the background. Which was exactly where he preferred it these days.

"I'd like a cosmopolitan," A woman at the bar behind him ordered. "with olives."

Who ordered olives with their cosmopolitans?

The server said something he couldn't understand. And the woman laughed.

Noah froze. Then in slow motion lifted his head and turned enough to see the woman in the red suit.

She had not been a vision. She was Savannah Skye Richards. His college sweetheart all grown up.

He'd recognized her, but his mind had refused to accept the reality that after twenty years, she'd be standing in front of him.

Closing his iPad, he laid it on the table and silently turned his chair around so he could watch her. He leaned back, his six-foot frame appearing relaxed – disguising the cat-like tension coursing through him.

She hadn't spotted him yet. Her gaze was glued to her phone – her fingers typing rapidly. The years had been good to her. She'd always been pretty, but now... she was drop-dead gorgeous. There was an air about her that hadn't been there when she was struggling in college. She carried an air of assurance and confidence now that hadn't been there before.

Twenty years. Then twice random crossings in less than an hour. It was more than he could ignore.

She must have felt him watching her. She glanced up, typed a couple of key-strokes. Then looked up again. He could tell by the way the corners of her mouth twitched the moment his presence registered with her. With her new self-assurance, he was certain that only he could tell. He'd spent, after all, countless hours studying her. For nearly a whole year.

Their gazes locked. He smiled. God, but it was good to see her.

Déjà vu was an understatement.

He'd been working registration his senior year. She was a freshman. Her first day on campus at Auburn University in Auburn, Alabama. He'd taken one look at her and fallen head over heels.

This time, however, instead of smiling, she was looking... displeased to see him.

He stood up, closed the distance between them, and sat at the bar next to her. "What brings you to this gin joint?" he said.

"Work," she said, clicking off her iPhone.

"It's been awhile," he said.

"Twenty years," she said, as the server set her cosmopolitan in front of her. She picked it up. Sipped.

"What are the odds?" he asked.

"I don't believe in chance." She kept her eyes focused on her drink.

"I guess a date at the casino is out."

She scoffed. "A date is out."

"Savannah Skye," he said.

"Savannah," she corrected.

He rubbed his chin. "Savannah. Look at me," She lifted her eyes and he saw a glimpse of the pain before she checked it.

"It's been twenty years since we saw each other. Let's at least say hello."

"Hello," she said.

"That's better."

She scowled again. "You started it."

He shook his head. "You're right. I did. I'm sorry. I was caught off guard."

She smiled, albeit a little wobbly. "I'm sorry, too. I've seen you twice in one day. That can't be coincidence."

"I agree," he said. "You look good. You look like I imagined."

She raised an eyebrow. "You imagined me."

He chuckled. "On occasion, yes."

"You're married," she pointed out, nodding toward his ring finger.

He glanced down. Saw the line on his ring finger, no more than a shadow to most. She always had been observant. "Divorced. Separated actually."

"Right," she said, looking at him askance. "Aren't you all?"

"What?"

She shrugged.

"It seems you've been hanging around the wrong crowd."

"Is that so? When's your divorce hearing date?"

"I don't know."

She rolled her eyes. Sipped her drink.

"Seriously. It's uncontested. I'm not even sure we have to go."

She glanced at him. Unlocked her phone.

"Ok. Here," he said, taking his own phone out of his pocket. "Let's call Matthew. Let's call my attorney."

"Let's don't."

"Why are you so interested in my marital state?"

"Ok, let's say for now I believe you."

"No, really, why are you?"

Her gaze met his now. She chuckled. "You've already asked me out."

"I most certainly did not."

"The casino," she said, locking her phone again.

He shook his head, "It's a figure of speech. When did you become so literal?"

She leaned back. Sighed. "After being hit on about five hundred times."

"Admirable," he said, "I can see the attraction."

She laughed. "Not like that. As part of my job."

He considered her in a different light now. Her clothes were much too fine for a stripper. Definitely not a prostitute.

"You're an escort?"

She sighed. "I see you never developed a filter."

He shrugged. "Some things never change."

"I'm not a call girl." She glared at him. "Or a prostitute. So don't get any ideas."

"I think you're about twenty-one years late on that request."

"Yeah, well, you're married now."

"Separated."

"Same thing."

"You're difficult. I'm impressed. What about you?"

He'd yet to get a glimpse of her ring finger. Truthfully, he'd been too enthralled to even think to look.

She held up her unadorned hand.

"Divorced?"

"Never married."

"Are you telling me that you never..." He trailed off. This conversation was completely unfair. He had no way to know what damage he'd done to her all those years ago.

"I work a lot."

He nodded. Self-sufficient. Successful. Hence the air of confidence. "What kind of work?"

"I'm a drug rep."

"Really?" Not at all what he expected.

"You may recall I was a science major."

"I do recall. And I'm sure you excelled."

"You could say that."

He smiled to himself. She had that slightly pouty expression that had always worked on him.

"I'm a pilot," he said, before he could stop himself.

She laughed. A genuine laugh now. Her green eyes twinkled with sincerity.

And it was in that moment. Just like that, that the years fell away and he was that college senior all over again. In love with the freshman coed.

"I never would have guessed."

"Did the uniform give me away?"

"That and the unerring devotion you put toward achieving that goal."

He sat a little taller in his chair. "You're successful at this drug rep thing you do," he said.

She tilted her head with a little smile. "I suppose. Why would you say that?"

"Because you're good at everything you do and..." he lifted one eyebrow suggestively. "You have a way of making a man do whatever it is you want."

She shook her head. The smile disappeared back into the little pout. "That seems a little odd coming from you." A silent message appeared on her phone. She checked it and pushed her unfinished drink aside.

"I'm sorry," she said.

She had managed to do it again. She had mesmerized him and he had no idea what she was talking about. "Sorry about what?"

"I have to go."

"Go?" He checked his watch. Such a short time had passed since he'd come into the club... yet his life, it seemed, had been altered forever.

The girl he had spent twenty years wondering about. Twenty years with a love in his heart that hadn't died.

And here she was. In the flesh.

"Yes," she said, with the flash of a smile at the corner of her lips. "I have a flight to catch." She stood up.

"Of course you do." *Why else would she be here?* For a mere moment in time, he'd allowed himself to think that she was there in his world just for him. Just for him and no one else.

She stood up. Pushed her chair to the bar. "It was good to see you again, Noah," she said, her lips curved in a polite smile no doubt used successfully when working with doctors.

"It was good to see you, too," he said, automatically.

She held out her hand.

He took her hand, but didn't shake it as she had obviously intended, but held it. Stared into those mesmerizing green eyes. She pulled back almost imperceptibly. He held tighter. Felt a gut-wrenching juxtaposition of familiar and new as she gave in and squeezed back. Just for a moment.

A moment in time. When his heart was light and the world narrowed down to them. Just the two of them.

"I'm gonna miss my flight," she said, pulling back in earnest now.

He released her. "Go," he said.

She picked up her bag and turned. Took a step.

His heart sank. Heavy again.

"Wait," he said, out of his chair in a flash and closing the distance between them. Stepping in front of her.

She raised an eyebrow.

"How will I find you?"

Her lips curved into a smug little smile. The smile he'd seen her wear after she aced a chemistry exam. "Perhaps we'll bump into each other again," she said.

"No," he insisted. "It's been twenty years. We both travel all the time. Right? You travel?"

"A fair amount."

"Well, you don't believe in chance. Yet in one day, we've bumped into each other twice... in one hour."

She shrugged. "What are the odds?"

He scoffed. "Out of the mouth of the one who doesn't believe in chance."

"I believe in science."

"Well, scientifically, we could never see each other again."

"You could always look for me this time."

He absorbed the jab. Owned it. "I could. I will. But the world is a big place."

She seemed to consider. Squinted into his eyes. Searching for something only she knew to look for.

"New York."

"New York what?"

"I'll be in New York for the next five days."

"Ha. New York doesn't narrow the world by very much."

She nodded. "It is a big city. But you know enough about me to find me."

"Wait," he said. "Until Monday?"

"Tuesday."

"Come on," he said. She turned. Smiled over her shoulder. That smile that had once been reserved only for him.

"See you around," she said, and walked away from him. He watched her walk through the door.

And took a deep steadying breath. Glanced at his watch. Now was not the time for a panic attack. He had a plane to fly in less than an hour.

Keep Reading Begin Again...

Kathryn Kaleigh writes sweet contemporary romance, time travel romance, and historical romance.

kathrynkaleigh.com

www.ingramcontent.com/pod-product-compliance
Lightning Source LLC
Chambersburg PA
CBHW051410130726
47987CB00007B/2933